OUR FAVORITE FOODS

Grilled Cheese Sandwiches

by Joanne Mattern

BLASTOFF! READERS 3

BELLWETHER MEDIA • MINNEAPOLIS, MN

Blastoff! Readers are carefully developed by literacy experts to build reading stamina and move students toward fluency by combining standards-based content with developmentally appropriate text.

 Level 1 provides the most support through repetition of high-frequency words, light text, predictable sentence patterns, and strong visual support.

 Level 2 offers early readers a bit more challenge through varied sentences, increased text load, and text-supportive special features.

 Level 3 advances early-fluent readers toward fluency through increased text load, less reliance on photos, advancing concepts, longer sentences, and more complex special features.

★ **Blastoff! Universe**

Reading Level

This edition first published in 2021 by Bellwether Media, Inc.

No part of this publication may be reproduced in whole or in part without written permission of the publisher. For information regarding permission, write to Bellwether Media, Inc., Attention: Permissions Department, 6012 Blue Circle Drive, Minnetonka, MN 55343.

Library of Congress Cataloging-in-Publication Data

Names: Mattern, Joanne, 1963- author.
Title: Grilled Cheese Sandwiches / by Joanne Mattern.
Description: Minneapolis, MN : Bellwether Media, Inc., 2021. | Series: Blastoff! Readers | Includes bibliographical references and index. | Audience: Ages 5-8 | Audience: Grades 2-3 | Summary: "Simple text and full-color photography introduce beginning readers to grilled cheese sandwiches. Developed by literacy experts for students in kindergarten through third grade"-Provided by publisher.
Identifiers: LCCN 2020036796 (print) | LCCN 2020036797 (ebook) | ISBN 9781644874349 | ISBN 9781648341113 (ebook)
Subjects: LCSH: Sandwiches--Juvenile literature. | Cooking (Cheese)--Juvenile literature.
Classification: LCC TX759.5.C48 M38 2021 (print) | LCC TX759.5.C48 (ebook) | DDC 641.6/73--dc23
LC record available at https://lccn.loc.gov/2020036796
LC ebook record available at https://lccn.loc.gov/2020036797

Text copyright © 2021 by Bellwether Media, Inc. BLASTOFF! READERS and associated logos are trademarks and/or registered trademarks of Bellwether Media, Inc.

Editor: Kieran Downs   Designer: Brittany McIntosh

Printed in the United States of America, North Mankato, MN.

Table of Contents

Gooey and Tasty	4
Grilled Cheese Sandwich History	8
Grilled Cheese Sandwiches Today	14
Glossary	22
To Learn More	23
Index	24

Gooey and Tasty

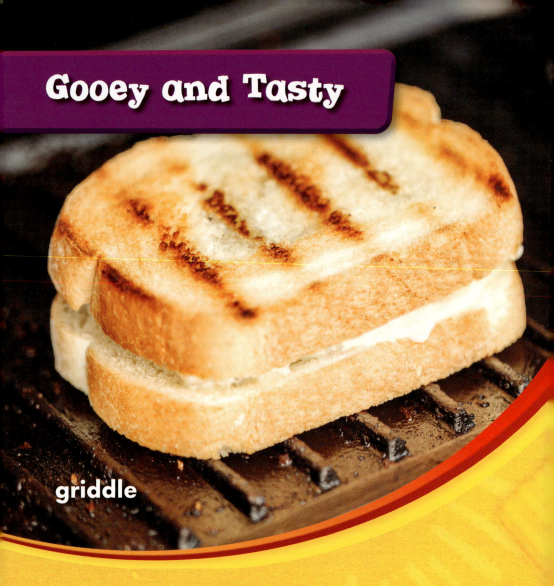

griddle

Buttered bread crackles against the hot **griddle**. Melted cheese oozes between the slices of bread. Time to eat!

Grilled cheese sandwiches are a favorite American meal.

Grilled cheese sandwiches are simple. They have cheese, butter, and two slices of bread.

How to Make a Grilled Cheese Sandwich

1. Butter one side of two slices of bread
2. Place cheese between the slices of bread
3. Toast both sides of the sandwich in a hot pan
4. Eat and enjoy!

When the sandwich is grilled, the cheese melts. This makes a hot, tasty meal.

Grilled Cheese Sandwich History

People have eaten cheese and bread together for thousands of years. In **ancient** Rome, people ate cheese and bread as a meal.

But the heated sandwich was created in the early 1900s in the United States.

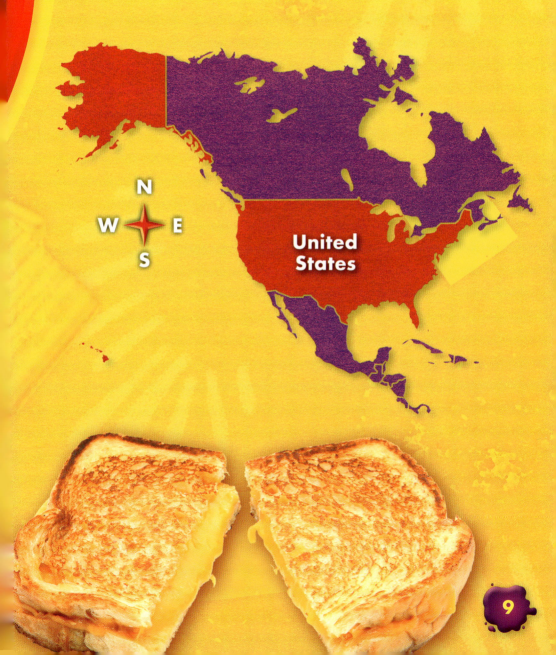

Easy Grilled Cheese

Ask an adult to help you make your own grilled cheese sandwich!

Tools

- frying pan or griddle
- spatula

Ingredients

- 2 slices of bread
- 2 slices of cheese
- butter

Instructions

1. Heat a pan or griddle on the stove.
2. Spread butter on one side of both slices of bread.
3. Place one piece of bread buttered side down in the pan. Be careful!
4. Place the cheese on top of the slice of bread that is in the pan.
5. Place the second piece of bread on top of the sandwich with the buttered side facing out.
6. Cook until both sides are golden brown and the cheese is melted. Flip the sandwich as needed.

bread slicer

Otto Rohwedder

James Kraft

In 1906, James Kraft made cheese that did not **spoil**. Otto Rohwedder invented a machine to slice bread in 1928. During the **Great Depression**, these cheap **ingredients** became popular. People heated them together to make toasted cheese sandwiches.

open-faced grilled cheeses

Early grilled cheeses were open-faced. They included **shredded** cheese. Some people heated them in ovens.

Eventually, people started using griddles to heat them. In the 1960s, the sandwiches became known as grilled cheeses.

Grilled Cheese Timeline

1906
James Kraft invents cheese that does not spoil

1928
Otto Rohwedder invents the bread slicer

1960s
Toasted bread and cheese are called grilled cheese sandwiches

Grilled Cheese Sandwiches Today

Today, people eat grilled cheese sandwiches at home. Restaurants serve them, too.

There is even a National Grilled Cheese Day! It is celebrated on April 12.

bauru

rarebit

Styles of grilled cheeses are found around the world. *Bauru* is made in Brazil. It is a soft bun with cheese, meat, and vegetables.

Rarebit is made in Wales by pouring cheese sauce over toast.

Grilled Cheese Sandwiches Around the World

France

croque monsieur

Italy

panini

Mexico

quesadilla

England

toastie

American cheese is a favorite on grilled cheeses. **Cheddar** and **mozzarella** are popular, too.

grilled cheese with cheddar

grilled cheese with mozzarella

grilled cheese on French bread

grilled cheese on a bagel

Grilled cheeses can be made with sliced bread. They can also be made with French bread. Even a bagel works. Anything goes!

Many people make at least one grilled cheese sandwich a month. Some people add foods like meat or vegetables to their sandwich. Grilled cheeses are often paired with tomato soup. These sandwiches are a great meal!

Crunchy Nacho Grilled Cheese

Add some crunch and spice to your sandwich! Ask an adult to help you make this tasty meal.

Tools

- frying pan or griddle
- spatula

Ingredients

- 2 slices of bread
- 2 slices of cheese
- butter
- sliced jalapeño peppers
- crushed corn chips or nacho cheese chips

Instructions

1. Heat a pan or griddle on the stove.
2. Spread butter on one side of both slices of bread.
3. Place one piece of bread buttered side down in the pan.
4. Add the cheese slices, sliced jalapeño peppers, and crushed chips.
5. Place the second piece of bread on top of the sandwich with the buttered side facing out.
6. Cook until both sides are golden brown and the cheese is melted. Flip the sandwich as needed.

Glossary

ancient—a long time ago

cheddar—a firm, smooth, yellow or orange cheese

Great Depression—a period of time from the late 1920s through the 1930s when people did not have a lot of money

griddle—a flat iron plate used to cook food

ingredients—foods that are combined to make another food

mozzarella—a mild, soft, white cheese

shredded—cut or torn into long, narrow strips

spoil—to go bad

styles—ways something is done

To Learn More

AT THE LIBRARY

Carroll, Ricki. *Say Cheese! A Kid's Guide to Cheese Making with Recipes for Mozzarella, Cream Cheese, Feta, and Other Favorites.* North Adams, Mass.: Storey Publishing, 2018.

Heos, Bridget. *From Milk to Cheese.* Mankato, Minn.: Amicus, 2018.

Leaf, Christina. *Macaroni & Cheese.* Minneapolis, Minn.: Bellwether Media, 2020.

ON THE WEB

Factsurfer.com gives you a safe, fun way to find more information.

1. Go to www.factsurfer.com.

2. Enter "grilled cheese sandwiches" into the search box and click 🔍.

3. Select your book cover to see a list of related content.

Index

bauru, 16
Brazil, 16
bread, 4, 6, 8, 19
bread slicer, 11
butter, 4, 6
cheese, 4, 6, 7, 8, 11, 12, 16, 17, 18
Great Depression, 11
griddle, 4, 13
history, 8, 9, 11, 12, 13
how to make, 6
ingredients, 11
Kraft, James, 11
meal, 5, 7, 8, 20
meat, 16, 20
National Grilled Cheese Day, 14
ovens, 12

rarebit, 16, 17
recipe, 10, 21
restaurants, 14
Rohwedder, Otto, 11
Rome, 8
styles, 16, 17
timeline, 13
tomato soup, 20
United States, 9
vegetables, 16, 20
Wales, 17

The images in this book are reproduced through the courtesy of: Dani Vincek, front cover, p. 3; Arina P Habich, p. ; Olga Miltsoa, pp. 5, 8, 18 (top), 22; Africa Studio, p. 6 (step 1); Colleen Michaels, p. 6 (step 2); MSPhotographic, pp. 6 (step 3), 7, 17 (quesadilla); fishwork, p. 6 (step 4); endeavor, p. 9; Michael C. Gray, p. 10; AntiD, p. 11 (bread slicer); Pictorial Press Ltd / Alamy Stock Photo, p. 11 (Rohwedder); Unknown / Wikipedia, p. 11 (Kraft); Monkey Business Images, p. 12; ALEAIMAGE, p. 14; Funwithfood, p. 15; MarcosMartinezSanchez, p. 16 (top); threerocksimages, p. 16 (bottom); Tanya_F, p. 17 (croque monsieur); Karl Allgaeuer, p. 17 (panini); VISION4RY-L4NGU4GE, p. 17 (toastie); Mariha-kitchen, p. 18 (bottom); Maxim Khytra, p. 19 (top); Flopaganifoto, p. 19 (bottom); Brent Hofacker, p. 20; Kieran Downs, p. 21.